BIG ERNIE'S NEW HOME

A Story for Children Who Are Moving

by Teresa and Whitney Martin

MAGINATION PRESS • WASHINGTON, D.C.

Published by
MAGINATION PRESS
An Educational Publishing Foundation Book
American Psychological Association
750 First Street, NE
Washington, DC 20002

For more information about our books, including a complete catalog, please write to us,
call 1-800-374-2721, or visit our website at www.maginationpress.com.

Editor: Darcie Conner Johnston
Designer: Susan K. White
The text type is Hadriano
Printed by Phoenix Color, Rockaway, New Jersey

Library of Congress Cataloging-in-Publication Data

Martin, Teresa.
Big Ernie's new home : a story for children who are moving / by Teresa and Whitney Martin.
p. cm.
ISBN 1-59147-382-9 (hardcover : alk. paper) — ISBN 1-59147-383-7 (pbk. : alk. paper)
1. Moving, Household—Juvenile literature. I. Martin, Whitney, 1968- II. Title.
TX307.M38 2006
648'.9—dc22
2005027069

10 9 8 7 6 5 4 3 2 1

For our little movers
Roddy, Whitney, Ernie, Ella, and Pablo
All our love, Mommy and Daddy

In an old house, on a steep hill,
there once lived a very brave cat.
His name was Ernie.
Everyone called him Big Ernie.

Big Ernie lived with a little boy named Henry.
Every morning Little Henry made Big Ernie a delicious tuna breakfast.
And after breakfast, they always went for their morning adventure.
Even when it rained in winter.

Big Ernie was not scared of anything.
Not even flying dragons.

One time he even rode in a cable car.

Every afternoon,
after the fog disappeared,
Big Ernie curled up
in his favorite green chair.
He drifted off to faraway places.

At night, when the streetlights started to hum,
Big Ernie liked to play with his best friend, Pablo.

After a game of cat and mouse, Big Ernie snuggled into his nighttime place.

He said goodnight to the cowboy riding into the sunset.

He said goodnight to the flying red dragon hanging on three strings.

And he said goodnight to Pablo, sleeping among Little Henry's things.

Big Ernie was very happy.

He was happy until one especially foggy morning,

when Little Henry said,

"We aren't taking a walk today, Big Ernie.

It's time to put our toys in boxes.

Today we're moving to a new home."

Boxes and boxes and more boxes
appeared everywhere Big Ernie went.
"It's time to stop playing," said Little Henry.
"It's time to put Pablo in a box.
Don't worry. He'll be okay."

Little Henry picked up Big Ernie and said, "It's time for us to say goodbye now."
"Goodbye ocean waves. Goodbye trees. Goodbye cable cars.
Goodbye bridge. Goodbye streetlight. And goodbye house."

After saying goodbye, Big Ernie saw IT.

THE RED BOX.

The red box meant only one thing.

Dr. Shep's office.

OH, NO!

"Oh, Ernie," said Little Henry,

"we're not going to the doctor's office.

This is a different kind of trip.

Today we're moving to our new home."

The car passed by the doctor's office.

Big Ernie meowed loudly,

"Where are we going?

What's a 'new home'?"

When the car door finally opened, Big Ernie knew he was in a new place.

He couldn't feel the rain and fog against his whiskers.

He couldn't smell the dinner rolls baking at Wong's.

He couldn't hear the bells ringing on the cable cars.

All he could hear was the whisper of the wind on his fur.

Ernie was a little worried. He wasn't feeling so "Big" in this new place.

Little Henry crouched down by Big Ernie. He said, "There are a lot of wonderful things to see and do here. Let's start with one of our favorites, a tuna breakfast."

Big Ernie needed to eat a lot of tuna breakfasts before feeling big enough to take his morning adventure. Then one day, after an especially delicious meal, Little Henry and Big Ernie stepped outside their door. SLOOOWLY. VEERRRY SLOOOWLY.

"Big Ernie, say hello to Santa Fe. This is our new home," announced Little Henry.

NEW HOME? How could this be home?

The colors were all wrong. Everything was brown and white.

Where were the red dragons? Big green trees? Blue ocean waves?

Everything smelled like chili. Where was the wonderful smell of fish?

And everything felt different, too. There wasn't even a sidewalk.

Big Ernie didn't like the cold, wet snow on his paws.

This couldn't be home.

Big Ernie was mad, and a little sad.
He had trouble sleeping.
He meowed all day and paced around the house.
Sometimes he even got into the red box,
hoping it would take him back to his old house.

Little Henry held Big Ernie tightly and said, "Ernie, I know you've been a little worried about living somewhere new. But you're still the Big Ernie. Even here."

Every morning, Little Henry brought Big Ernie his favorite tuna breakfast.
After their meal, Little Henry would take Big Ernie outside for their morning walk.
Every afternoon, Little Henry helped Big Ernie curl up on his favorite green chair for a nap.
And every evening, Little Henry tucked Big Ernie into his nighttime place.

Little by little, Big Ernie started to look,
really look, around his new home.
At first all he could see was the brown and white.
But then he began to see adventures all around him.

He saw a familiar dragon peeking out from under an old cable car.
Maybe they have dragons and cable cars in Santa Fe, too.

Big Ernie smelled big-eared rabbits. They were playing cat
and mouse in the snow. Maybe they would let him play, too.

He heard the sweet music of water running.
The river wasn't big, but it did have a bridge to look over!

Big Ernie began to feel better.

When the sun went down,
Big Ernie snuggled up next to Little Henry in his nighttime place.
He said goodnight to the cowboy riding into the sunset.
He said goodnight to his flying red dragon hanging on three strings.
And he said goodnight to Pablo, sleeping among Little Henry's things.

The next morning, Big Ernie was waiting
to start their morning adventure.
He was ready for anything.
Even a new home.

Note to Parents
by Jane Annunziata, Psy.D.

Moving is a very big deal for kids. It's especially hard for younger children who haven't developed the cognitive and emotional resources to cope. Even a short move around the corner requires a lot of adjustment, but the more new things a child must adapt to, the greater the stress. Moves that are farther away are harder, since everything in the child's physical world — parks, preschool, grocery store — changes. A move to a different climate (such as Florida to Minnesota) or a different setting (city, suburbs, small town, or rural) also presents extra challenges.

The Child's View

Young children haven't had life experiences to prepare them for these changes. With less knowledge to draw from or plug in to, they react more than older children or adults might.

Also, because they are less intellectually developed, they rely more on their senses to process the world around them, and so are more sensitive to changes in sights, smells, sounds, light, and temperature. Even the water can taste different. The more sensory changes involved in the move, the more jarring it will be.

It's important for parents to remember that even when they view the move as positive, their child rarely does. A bigger or nicer home, a room of his own, a bigger backyard, more playmates, a parent who is home more because of a reduced commute—these things seldom override the feelings of stress and loss. Young children are very attached to the places and people in their lives. With this degree of attachment come corresponding feelings of loss when the attachments are disrupted, regardless of the compensations.

Finally, young children have trouble grasping the notion of permanence. No matter how well a move may be explained, they are likely to ask when they are going back to their old house. Over time, children mature cognitively and realize what it means for something to be permanent. They also put down roots in their new surroundings and slowly develop feelings of attachment. The good news, then, is that children eventually come to accept their new house as their home.

Explaining the Move

Before giving your child the news, let her know that you have something important to talk about. This allows her to be more emotionally prepared. If yours is a two-parent household, both parents should share the news, as this sends the message that everyone is in it together.

Keep your explanation simple, clear, and geared to your child's level of under-standing. You could start with: "We have something important to talk to you about. There's a change coming up in our family. Mom is going to have a new job, and we are going to move to a new house near her new job. We know this will be a big change, even for Skipper! But we're excited about it too."

Address any of your child's questions or reactions, and in later conversations, slowly provide more and more age-appropriate information. Follow your child's lead in deciding how much detail to give and when.

Timing the News

The timing of the news is as important as how you relay it. The goal is to provide ample time for your child to prepare emotionally, while not telling so far in advance that the waiting seems to go on forever, creating more time to worry about it. For many preschoolers, two months is a good guideline, but consider your own child's needs. Children who have trouble transitioning will need more time than those who transition easily.

Make the time frame as concrete as possible by anchoring the move to things kids can understand, such as weather or holidays.

You might say, "It's spring now and the weather is just starting to get warm. We'll be moving at the beginning of summer, when it's really warm outside and we can go swimming and wear our shorts."

Anything else you can do to make it more concrete will help. Many preschoolers are familiar with calendars, for example. Your child can draw a circle around Moving Day and cross off the days or apply stickers as days pass. This will help him feel more in control of this very out-of-control life experience.

Reactions and Feelings

Be sure that children are given permission to have and express their full range of "moving" feelings—even the negative ones. When parents listen and help their children label and understand their feelings, the child is better able to navigate through them. Here are some common feelings that children experience:

- Loss. So many losses come with moving: house, bedroom, preschool, daycare, and more.
- Loss of control. Kids feel a total loss of control, expressed as: "No one asked me if I wanted to move!"
- Sadness. Grief is related to all of the loss involved in moving.
- Anxiety. This is a normal reaction to uncertainty.
- Anger. Anger results from all of the losses. Also, it can be an unconscious mask; the child stays busy with anger to keep the more upsetting feelings of sadness and anxiety at bay.

- Regression. Whining, backsliding in toileting habits, baby talk, and being oppositional are all normal reactions.
- Excitement! Last but not least, when kids are well prepared, they can feel some excitement about the things they do have to look forward to.

Reducing Stress

Parents can do many things to help their children adjust. If they seem to be having unusual difficulty with feelings of sadness or anger, do consult with your child's pediatrician or a mental health professional. In general, though, here are a number of things that parents can do to ease the process for everyone.

To begin with, introduce children to their new house and neighborhood before the move. If distance doesn't allow for that, show them pictures.

Create a gradual entry. Walk around the new preschool or daycare center before your child starts attending. Slowly familiarize him with the places and people he'll be getting to know.

As much as possible, keep the same things and routines in the new home: the same furnishings, the same activities, the same schedule.

Label regressive behavior and wonder aloud with your child about its connection to the move: "Maybe you're having a hard time using your four-year-old voice because you're upset about moving. Let's talk about what's bothering you, and you can make a picture of your feelings. I think that will help."

Help your child get involved in her new community by finding one or two activities outside of daycare or preschool

that she enjoyed in her old setting.

Give your child as much control as possible. Make sure he gets some say in the decoration of his room, the play equipment in the yard, and so forth.

Help your child keep her connections to people. Send a picture she makes, a photo, or a note or email that she dictates to you to an old babysitter, friend, or teacher. This will help her be more open to new people.

Help your child make a scrapbook with photos of his old home, room, and neighborhood. Include captions (and feelings!) that your child dictates to you. This is a helpful emotional outlet.

Enthusiasm is contagious. Communicate your own excitement!

Adjusting to a new home is a process that takes time, sometimes a full year or more. Reassure your children — and yourselves! — that this getting-to-know-you stage is normal. Some days will be better than others. Lend your children your optimism when they seem a little discouraged. Always acknowledge their feelings of loss, anger, and worry, but end your talks in a positive way. Your children will take their cues from you.

JANE ANNUNZIATA, PSY.D., is a clinical psychologist with a private practice for children and families in McLean, Virginia. She is also the author of many books and articles addressing the concerns of children and their parents.

Teresa and Whitney Martin
have recently survived moving to Santa Fe
with their two boys, two cats, and puppy.
This is their first book together,
after seventeen years of talking about it.